Babru The Pirate

The Orange Obelisk

Author:
Bruce Nadeau

Illustrator:
Bruce Nadeau

Editor and Publisher:
Jeffrey McGraw

Presented by:
BNJM Studios

Find BNJM Studios on Facebook

Also from Bruce Nadeau:

Babru the Pirate…
- 2015 The Silver Pipe Adventure
- 2016 The Orange Obelisk
- The Wedding Day Tale
- The Riddle of the Sphinx

Eden Glen Chronicles…
- 2015 The Last Unicorn
- 2017 The Great Sea Dragon

The Calabash Kids and...
- 2015 The Dragon's Claw

Tales Not To Go To Sleep With

Acknowledgements

Bruce would like to thank Zayana and Simon, who continue to inspire me. And to Robin who was more concerned with this book being right than hurting my feelings.

Jeff would like to thank his parents for introducing him to books at a young age and teaching me how to dream.

Babru sat in the Captain's stateroom of *The Falabula,* the pirate ship docked in the harbor, sipping juice from a pineapple through his silver pipe, and looking down at the items that covered his desk. He thought about the time that he and the crew had spent here in Aransas Pass fondly, but felt that it was time to move on. They still had a goodly pile of gold from the pink whale's belly, and had earned a small fortune selling the jewels and other valuables they had retrieved as well. At least they sold most of the jewels.

A small pile of colorful precious stones sat in the center of Babru's desk, next to an old leather-bound book written in Latin. He occasionally picked up the jewels and let them fall through his fingers to the desk. Two emeralds and three rubies repeatedly clattered on the table top.

"Hee, hee, hee," answered Babru. "That is a beautiful collection Captain," said Zayda from the doorway, "but you still haven't told us what they're for."

"You're not even going to tell me?" asked the pixie.

"Di, di, di," said Babru.

"Really?" asked Zayda surprised. "You have all of those gems, and the collection isn't complete? What else do you think you need?"

"Obulabula" said Captain Babru with a grin.

Zayda couldn't believe her ears. "But Captain, no one even knows for sure if that really exists."

Babru looked at the gems in his hand and smiled. He picked up a velvet bag with a draw string, and poured the gems in. He tied the bag to his belt and pointed out toward the ship's deck and said, "da, da, da!"

Zayda nodded and said, "Of course Captain, I'll assemble the crew, but they'll never believe this."

Out in the hot sun the crew gathered around the bridge awaiting the Captain's orders. As much as they enjoyed their stay at the seaside village, they were all eager for another adventure, especially if there were riches to be had. Captain Babru walked out on to the bridge, and Zayda fluttered out after him.

Babru waved his arms and said, "Obulabula."

The crew all nodded to each other, even though they still needed Zayda to translate for them. She fluttered up to the railing and looked over the crew. "Men, Captain Babru says we're on the hunt for...The Orange Obelisk!"

"But what is an obelisk?" asked Big Nose Pete.

"I can answer that question Miss Zayda," said the ship's handy man Carpenter Cal. "An obelisk is a tall, thin structure with four sides, ending in a pyramid on the top. They usually stand at least seventy feet tall, but some are considerably taller than that."

There was a clamor among the men and Big Nose Pete stepped forward again. "Miss Zayda, what is The Orange Obelisk?"

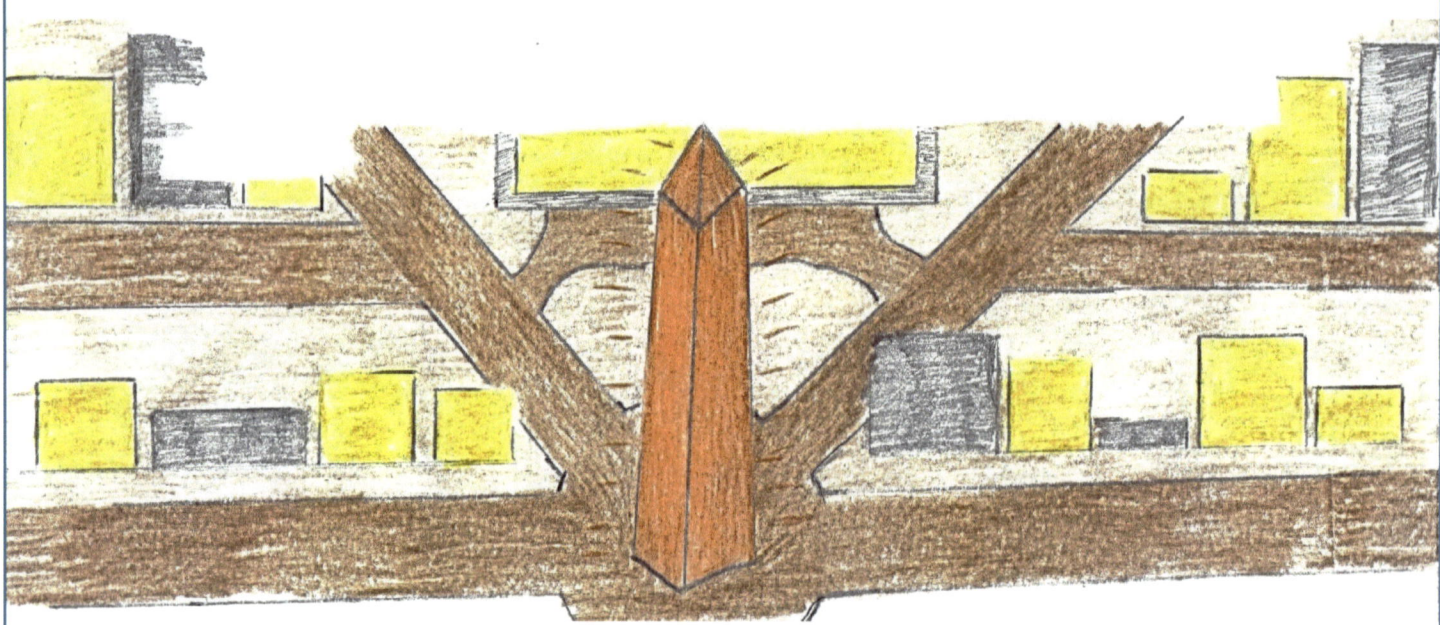

"Well Pete," began the pixie, "thoughts on that subject are tricky at best. The legend says that the only son of an Egyptian Pharaoh was given the gift of a model of the city of Thebes. The base was carved of sandstone, the buildings were made from gold and silver, but the true feature of this model was The Orange Obelisk. It stood taller than the other buildings in the model, maybe a foot long, and was made of a very rare orange tinted diamond."

"That must be worth a fortune," said Dog Face John.

"It would be worth more than that Dog Face," said Zayda. "If it was real."

"It isn't real, Miss Zayda?" he asked.

"Well, that's the tricky part. The model was destroyed, and taken apart when the Romans attacked the city. Most people think the diamond was cut into smaller pieces and given to members of the Roman Emperor's family. The Captain however, doesn't believe it, and thinks he knows where the obelisk is."

There were murmurs among the crew, and finally Big Nose Pete said, "Miss Zayda, Captain's been real good to us. If'n he thinks there's a treasure to be found, we're all in!" A cheer went up from the rest of the crew. Everyone quickly snapped to their jobs, and the ship was ready to go. They dropped the sails, tightened the lines, and with Captain Babru at the wheel, *The Falabula* cut out into the open water.

"All right men," cried the pixie. "We make our way up the coast. When we reach Boston Town we stock up on food and other provisions, then we make our voyage across the Atlantic."

Four-Eyed Fred, tightening one of the sail lines, asked, "We headed for Rome Miss Zayda?"

"Sorry Fred. That little bit of shiny may have been taken to Rome, but Captain thinks it's been taken from there too. We're headed north. Really north. We're off to Scandinavia."

"That far north?" asked Fred. "Why would the Captain think that?"

"Dum, du, dum, Uhoh!" said Captain Babru.

"Have you seen the book that the Captain purchased at the antiquities dealer in the bazaar?" asked Zayda. Four-Eyed Fred nodded and the pixie continued. "Well, the Emperor was apparently interested in other cultures and there history. It was written by a cleric that was sent to record the battle, and learn as much as he could about the Egyptian people. After his return to Rome, he was sent to the far north to learn about the Nordic People, their culture, and their rich mythology. In his notes it says:

> *I have learned not only of the people, but of the secret people that they fear. It is with this group that I have, in trade for my life, given that which lights their way.*

Captain Babru believes the cleric removed the obelisk from the model, never told the Emperor about it, and then took it with him to Scandinavia. While there he got in some sort of trouble, and had to trade the obelisk away to save his life. Captain believes that it's still there."

"So we're not just going to Scandinavia, are we?" asked Fred.

"Afraid not," answered Zayda. "We're going inland and up the mountains. We're looking for the people the Nordic people are afraid of, and we're going to take the obelisk away from them. I just hope the Captain has figured out how he's going to do it."

The ship sailed through the night, making its way north. When they sailed into Boston harbor Captain Babru and Zayda prepared the landing party. There was the Captain and the first mate, Carpenter Cal, Generous George the ships quartermaster, and Cooky the ship's cook. Their job was to bring on supplies for their cross Atlantic voyage. When they returned to the ship and loaded their purchases, it was time to head east.

It was a long voyage, but the men kept busy as best they could. They kept the ship clean, Zayda continued to give those men that were interested their reading lessons, and Carpenter Cal worked on the special project that Captain Babru had given him.

Suddenly Four-Eyed Fred called down from the crow's nest. "Captain! We got a ship like I've never seen before off the starboard bow!"

All the men that could ran to the rail and stared off towards the horizon. Not a one of them knew what to make of what they saw. Dog Face John uttered, "What manner of ship be that? It has no sails, no real shape, and seems to be crewless. And why is it entirely white?"

Zayda jumped up onto the rail between the men and said, "Men that is no ship. That is an iceberg." She immediately spun around and started shouting out commands. "All right men emergency positions! Spotters to the front of the ship, and stow the main sails. We need to slow ourselves down a bit. If there is one iceberg, there's bound to be more. The good news is we're right on course."

With Four-Eyed Fred spotting from the crow's nest, and Dog Face John and Big Nose Pete spotting from the front of the ship, they sailed towards the icebergs. Captain Babru steered the ship from the bridge with a sense of calmness, listening to his men describing the locations of the icebergs, and making adjustments in the ship's course. Soon the icebergs were behind them.

"LAND HO!" called Four-Eyed Fred, and everyone breathed a little easier. They had arrived. *The Falabula* sailed into the harbor and the crew prepared to head to shore.

"Captain, any idea who you want coming with us?" Zayda asked.

Captain Babru smiled and began pointing at crew members. Those that were selected didn't know why, but they trusted the Captain's judgment, and they got ready.

Big Nose Pete took a bag of gold coins from Generous George to conduct business in town. Carpenter Cal packed the thin boards that the Captain had asked him to prepare. They were sanded smooth and had leather straps attached to them. And Scottish Rob packed the Captains gear and lowered the landing boat.

"B,b,b,b,b," said Captain Babru as the group climbed onto the dock in town.

"You're right Captain," said Zayda. "It's very cold. Scottish Rob, take some gold coins. You need to find us a wagon and a couple of horses. Pete, get over to the clothiers, we're going to need some warm jackets. Cal, the Captain said you should get us ten lamps, and a barrel of lamp oil. We'll all meet back here."

The crew all headed off in different directions. There was one thing that pirates knew about harbor side towns. They were different because of their location, but they were all the same. Cal new gear shops were always located near the dock for last minute supplies before beginning a voyage. He had the lamps and oil in ten minutes.

Pete new clothiers were found next to inns. Inns were always located next to the taverns. And Taverns started right after you arrived in town at the dock. After a little haggling, and some searching for the correct sizes, he was ready to go.

Scottish Rob had the most trouble. Finding the stables was the easy part. They are always at the most inland edge of the town, but finding it wasn't the problem. After some negotiations he left with his purchases, worried that the Captain would be upset with what he had found.

The others had all gathered at the dock waiting for Scottish Rob to return with the wagon. They all wore their new jackets, hats, and gloves, and felt much warmer. There was a light ringing sound from the edge of town, and seemed to be getting louder. They all turned towards the sound, and Big Nose Pete said, "By the Pirate King's beard, that's no wagon, and thems is certainly not horses!"

Scottish Rob came to a stop in front of the crew and saw the shock on their faces. They looked over the wagon which had no wheels. It had long runners on the bottom, causing it to glide across the snow and ice, but the real surprise was the animals at the front. They were the size of good pack mules, but had huge sets of horns on their heads.

"Rob?" asked Zayda.

Scottish Rob cleared his throat as he put on his heavy coat, "Well Miss Zayda, it seems in these parts they don't use wagons, but what they call sleighs. No horses neither. These wee beasties are called reindeer, and the man at the stables says these lassies will be able to handle the snow, ice, and the mountains."

They looked to Captain Babru for approval, and he began to giggle as he climbed into the sleigh next to Scottish Rob. That was good enough for the rest of them so they loaded the sleigh. In went the lamps and oil. Pete added the extra blankets, and Cal grabbed the three planks of wood the Captain had him prepare. Babru felt along his belt to make sure he had the bag of jewels, and pointed up the mountain. Rob grabbed the reins and snapped the reindeer into action.

While they slowly made their way up the mountain, Zayda turned to Big Nose Pete. "Did you ask about the secret people Pete?"

"Aye Miss Zayda," answered Pete. "Scared him pretty bad. Says they aren't people at all. Monsters says he."

"Monsters?" asked Zayda.

"Aye," said Pete, "snow monsters! Seven feet tall, covered in fur with huge fangs that glow!"

Pete shivered and so did the pixie. "Do you think he could be correct Miss Zayda?"

"Captain doesn't seem worried Pete," said Zayda. "I just hope that he's right."

The higher they went, the more the wind blew, and the colder the air got. They were all huddled in the sleigh with the extra blankets wrapped around them when they heard it. A high pitched howl wailed in the distance. Scottish Rob began to rein in the deer, but Captain Babru pointed higher up the mountain. Another howl, closer this time, scared the crew. Babru put his hand on Rob's shoulder to calm him down, and pointed up the mountain. Suddenly movement from their left caught the group's attention.

Two huge figures stepped out from the tree line. They were huge beasts with their arms held up high. Covered entirely in fur, with their eyes almost completely hidden,

they had long fangs hanging from their mouths that seemed to glow. Their giant feet helped them move easily through the snow, and deep growly noises came from them as they approached the sleigh with their arms outstretched!

Big Nose Pete screamed.

Carpenter Cal screamed.

Scottish Rob screamed.

Zayda screamed.

Babru giggled and pointed to a small clearing at the end of the tree line.

Scottish Rob snapped the reins and the deer started to run. The sleigh cut through the snow and raced toward the clearing. As they came around the grove of thick pine trees, there was nothing in front of them but the sheer face of the mountain. With nowhere to go to the front, the group looked behind them. The two snow monsters had come around the trees and were heading right towards them.

"We're trapped!" yelled Scottish Rob.

A smiling Captain Babru tapped his arm and pointed at the mountain face to their left. Rob could see it now. Behind some large boulders and a patch of shrubbery, there was a cave. Rob headed the sleigh toward the opening. The shrubs and small trees next to the mouth of the cave created a natural shelter from the snow and wind, so he put the sleigh and reindeer under it, while everyone else ran into the cave. They ran into the darkness, but only felt safe for a minute. The light from the cave mouth was blotted out by the two huge figures that followed them into the cave.

They continued to run into the darkness trying to escape when they suddenly entered a cavern in the mountain. Despite the danger behind them, they stopped in disbelief at what lay in front of them. The cavern was huge. To the left was a net strung from the rock formations and covered with blankets, to the right was a small hearth with pots and pans on top. But the center of the room was what held their attention. Standing on a pedestal, in a shaft of sunlight that seemed to be coming from a small crack in the ceiling, stood The Orange Obelisk! The shaft of light hitting it caused it to shine and reflect the light everywhere, brightening the great room.

A groan from behind them reminded them of the danger, and they all jumped to find a hiding place. Pete and Cal jumped behind a rock. Zayda and Rob quickly ran into an adjoining tunnel. Babru stood in the middle of the room facing the tunnel the two monsters were coming through. When they entered the room they took two steps toward the tiny Captain, and he put out his hand.

The crew watched in horror as the great beasts approached the Captain. The monsters towered over the tiny Babru and reached down to grab him. Zayda couldn't watch. She screamed, "NOOOOOO!" and jumped out of her hiding spot, trying to protect her friend.

She froze however, confused, when the monster didn't grab him, but shook Babru's hand!

The second monster reached up and broke off it's teeth, and then pulled off its own head.

At least that is what it looked like to the crew. Actually, the teeth were just icicles hanging from the heavy hood, which was also pulled off. A woman shook out her long blond hair, while the other monster removed his head too.

"Jumpin' jiminy! It's cold out there! My goodness but it's nice to be back inside. Jorge Jorgenson's the name, this is my wife Inga. Who are you little fellow?"

"Babru!" said the captain, and pointing to the pixie with the confused expression, "Zayda!"

The other pirates came from their hiding spots, also confused, and introductions were made. Jorge shook all of their hands, and while Inga huddled them all near the fire to warm up, he said, "It's very nice to meet all of you, but why are you here, and why were you running away from us?"

"You were a-chasin' us," said Big Nose Pete. "You were moaning and howling, and your teeth was a-glowin."

Jorge laughed. "Young man we weren't howling." Grabbing a small horn tied to a small strap, he held it out to the pirates. "We were just blowing these horns. That's how we communicate up here."

"We?" asked Zayda.

"Of course. My Family has been living in these caves for hundreds of years. And our teeth weren't glowing. The icicles sparkle in the setting sun." Jorge turned to the Captain, "And now young man, what is it I can do for you?"

Captain Babru pointed at the orange diamond in the center of the room. "Obulabula!"

"It is nice," said Jorge, "but we need it to keep the room well lit."

Babru giggled and sent Big Nose Pete and Scottish Rob out to the sleigh for the lamps and oil. Once the lamps were lit Jorge couldn't help but shake his head and laugh.

"You know for all the years we've been coming up here, I've never thought of that! You have a deal young man, we'll take the lamps and oil, you can have that orange thing."

Babru smiled and put the Orange Obelisk in his pocket, but Zayda had some questions. "Excuse me Mr. Jorgenson, what did you mean "when you come up"?"

"Oh," said Jorge, "We live in town most of the year. We only come up for six weeks or so to get some work done. It used to take longer, but now that our sons are old enough to help with the work, we're done in no time."

"What kind of work do you do up here?" asked Zayda. "And why would you give up that diamond?"

"Why don't you kids come with Inga and me. I think I can answer both of those questions at the same time." Jorge grabbed one of the lamps and led everyone down the passage that Zayda and Rob had tried to hide in. At the end of the winding tunnel the area opened into a huge cavern. When Jorge held out the bright oil lamp the crew was dazzled by the view. From everywhere in the chamber light sparkled back at them.

The room was filed with diamonds! From floor to ceiling covering the walls were diamonds of every imaginable size and shape. "This is my families mine. As you can see, we have more diamonds then we could ever need."

Zayda suddenly understood the legends. "That's why you pretend to be monsters, to keep anyone else from finding this place."

"That's right young lady," said Jorge. "Not only do people stay away, but nobody from town ever comes up here and figures out who we are. It was my great-great-great-great-great grand pappy's idea."

Scottish Rob asked, "But don't the people in town get suspicious when you show up with a bag of diamonds?"

"Ha Ha," said Jorge. "Aw, we never sell them in town. My oldest boy, Logan Jorgenson, takes them to the town on the other side of the mountain. They open up on the Baltic Sea. From there it is easy for our agent to sell them to southern Europe and Asia. We have plenty of money and only work six weeks a year."

In exchange for keeping the Jorgenson's secret, Jorge allowed the pirates to fill their pockets with as many diamonds as they wanted. Babru however, was only interested in five pieces of broken black rock from the floor of the cave. The crew thanked Mrs. Jorgenson, put on their coats, and headed to the front of the cave to head down the mountain.

When they arrived at the opening to the cave, Zayda instructed Cal to unpack the planks and lay them out in the snow. When the sleigh was empty, Babru handed the reins to Jorge.

"Thank you young man," said Jorge. "I won't lie, it would be handy to have this sleigh and these animals up here, but how will you get back down the mountain without them?"

Babru just laughed and pointed to Carpenter Cal.

"It seems to me," said Zayda with a smile, "the Captain already has a plan, and it involves our new ship carpenter, Mr. Afornya. Isn't that right Cal?"

Cal Afornya shrugged his shoulders and smiled. He stepped up to the first of the planks lying in the snow, and slid his feet under the leather straps the Captain told him to attach. Captain Babru jumped onto his back, and they began sliding down the mountain. Scottish Rob did the same, and Zayda jumped on his shoulder. Big Nose Pete, a little less boldly, got on his plank on his hands and knees, and started off behind them. The Jorgenson family stood and waved from the mouth of the cave and the pirates shouted their good-byes as they sped down the mountain.

When they reached the bottom of the mountain, they were greeted by Dog Face John, and the other members of the crew from the ship. They told of the run in with the snow monsters (they had after all promised to keep the Jorgenson's secret), showed them their pockets full of diamonds, and described the thrill of racing down the mountain on Cal Afornya's "snow boards".

Dog Face John brought Zayda to a local café, and introduced her to a wonderful drink that the locals made. They called it hot chocolate, and Zayda agreed it was just perfect. Especially with the dollop of fresh whipped cream on top. After hearing the whole and true story of what happened on the mountain top (Dog Face John had been a pirate longer than anyone else in the crew, and could be trusted with secrets), he asked about Captain Babru.

"So, he found the Obelisk?"

"Yep," said Zayda.

"He ever tell you why he wanted the Obelisk, or that baggie of jewels on his belt?" asked John.

"You know Dog Face," answered Zayda, "he never did. What say you and I go find him and get some answers."

The two of them left a gold coin on the table to pay for the chocolate and service, pulled on their coats, and headed out of the café. They didn't find him near the docks, or at the Inn. They finally headed toward the town square when they heard a commotion. When they took the corner, they realized the commotion was laughter and play. The rest of the crew, Captain Babru included, were in the middle of an epic snowball battle.

Zayda looked in the direction that Babru was running from, and finally got her answers.

Lovingly she said, "Oh Babru," then ran off to join the crew.

Bruce lives in Peabody, Massachusetts with Mommy, the real life Babru, and Zayda, and Kingston. He hopes that they continue to enjoy Babru the Pirate for years to come. Look for Babru's next adventure, The Wedding Day Tales coming later in 2016...

Jeff lives north of Boston with his wife. They enjoy traveling to national parks and orienteering in the summer. He is excited about bringing stories to children of all ages.

www.ingramcontent.com/pod-product-compliance
Lightning Source LLC
Chambersburg PA
CBHW041012170626
46815CB00003B/272